About The Author

Greetings! My name is Nia Saffell and I am itching to make a difference! I am a first year teacher and a first time author. In my fieldwork, and my own experience, I have found that children of color are STILL marginalized and have little representation throughout their entire educational experience and that is what inspired me to get writing. In the same breath, children who are not of color have little to no opportunities or safe spaces to ask legitimate questions about the differences they notice. That ends with me. There can be no change without equipping the next generation, and THAT is my full time job and hobby!

DEDICATION

For my all of the strong women in my corner, encouraging me to continue to rise. For all of the black little girls and boys, embrace who you are and always shine bright like the stars you are. For my future children, I followed my dreams so that you can too, I love you.

One beautiful day, a sleepy headed girl named Renee, got shaken out of bed to begin her day. "Wake up Lazy Bones, it's time for school. Quickly! We need enough time to tackle that hair!" Mom expressed.

Renee walked sluggishly to the bathroom to start her
morning routine. "Okay Babycakes, how do you want your hair today ?"
asked Mom. Renee responded, "Can you make it straight?"
"Fine," Mom replied. "But don't start screamin' and hollerin'
when I have to comb it out. Deal?"
"Deal!" Renee said excitedly.

Mom flat ironed Renee's hair in a frenzy because they were running late.
"Ow, Mom that hurts!" said Renee. "Shush we had a deal! Besides,
we're almost done. Now, hold still so I can finish!" said Mom.

Renee grabbed her breakfast and headed straight for the car!
Mom drove as fast as she could, ZOOMING through
neighborhoods. "Have a great day at school Baby!"
shouted Mom, "and don't let people
play in your hair!"

Renee went through the day without a single soul touching her luxurious locks. Renee is waiting for her favorite part of the day, recess! Renee's teacher shouted, "Alright friends, the only thing left to do is play outside! Don't forget your homework!"

Everyone rushed outside. Renee spotted familiar faces, so she ran to them with excitement. "Wow Renee" said Emily, "your hair is really long." Stacy chimed in, "Yeah, is it your real hair? I've never seen you wear it like this before!". Renee began to get a little frustrated by her friends comments. "Please don't touch my hair, my mom says our gross hands should stay out of our lovely locks" replied Renee.

Renee remembered that mom said it is best to walk away when something bothers you, so Renee began to walk. Her friends followed and kept asking questions. "Well why does it feel like that?" said Emily. "Yeah, our hair feels silky and it feels like yours is completely different." Said Stacey. Renee was beginning to feel embarrassed for being different. "Well, I don't know, I guess I never thought about it," said Renee confused.

Renee hung her head low when she walked to the car.
She was sad and confused about why her friends asked so many questions
about something as simple as hair.
Mom noticed Renee feeling down when she got into the car.
"What's wrong Renee? Did you have a rough day at school?"
asked mom. Renee answered, "Why isn't my hair like everyone else's?
My hair should feel as silky, right? Instead,
it feels super different from my friend's hair."
Mom had to think for a second, "Well baby,
that is just how your hair is and there is nothing wrong with that.
Your hair is perfect, just like you!".

They finally pulled up to their house and Renee plopped herself out of the car. She went to her room and inspected her dolls. "Mom, I want my hair to look like THIS in the morning," said Renee. Mom took the doll and put it down. "Your hair is different and beautiful the way it is Babycakes. Get ready for bed," Mom said.

Every night, Renee prays before bed. Tonight, she had a special request, "Lord, I pray you make my hair beautiful. I want to look like my friends and have the same hair that they do. Amen" whispered Renee.

The bright sun peeked its beautiful face through the windows,
waking Renee up. She walked into Mom's room. Mom saw her
grouchy little face through the bathroom mirror. "Good morning Babycakes,"
Mom greeted Renee. "How do you want your hair today?" Renee wiped her eyes and
responded, "I'm having a monstrous hair day. Just do anything to fix
this mess Mom." "I'll sure try Love," Mom replied.
"I might have to grab the scissors!"
she joked. "What?!" Renee responded, shocked.
"Oh, I'm just kidding Grumpy Pants," laughed Mom.

They scrambled out of the door and went on their way to school.
Before Renee could get out of the car Mom said,
"I love you Babycakes. Have a good day,
and remember that you are beautiful!"

Renee sat in class with her head in her hands, thinking about what it would be like to be the same as everyone else. "Okay Class, before morning recess I want to introduce you to two new students Elaine and Robert! Make them feel welcomed at recess," Mrs. Holloway said.

Everyone rushed outside. Renee was eager to introduce herself and her friends to the new students. "Hey, I'm Renee, these are my friends Emily and Stacy. I really like your hair Elaine" Robert and Elaine turn around with a big smiles on their faces, "Thank you! Your hair looks nice too!" said Elaine happily. Renee's smile goes away and she looks at the ground, "No, it's not, it's too kinky." Robert and Elaine looked shocked at her answer. "So is mine but my mom always tells me it's Funkadelic and perfectly Fro-tabulous!" said Robert. "Just because our hair is different that does not mean it's not perfect!" said Robert. Elaine jumps in, "Yeah, my mom said that Black people come in all shades, shapes, and sizes, and our hair is no different! Besides, we have so many styles we can use with our hair, it's a huge part of our culture!". Renee's smile came back. "Wow, I didn't know hair could be so important! What styles can you guys do with your hair?", Stacy asked eagerly.

"Well to start off," said Elaine,
"there are so many types of braids
we can do. We can rock the fro, we can rock it straight,
we can rock it curly, we can rock it short, we can rock it
long, we can rock our hair anyway we want!"

Braids

Straight

Long

Curly

Short

"We also have different hair types and curl patterns!
I call my hair my crown because
I feel like a King the bigger it grows! "
exclaimed Robert. "I never thought about my hair like that
before. You guys taught me so much. I can't wait to tell my Mom.
I wonder if she knows as much as I do?!" said Renee.

The bell rang, and Renee was so excited to tell her mom about what she learned at school about her hair.
"Did you have a better day?" asked Mom.
"Oh yes, and some new friends taught me about my crown," said Renee "I am so happy to hear that, but what crown?" asked Mom. "My hair, it's called a crown and it makes me feel like a Queen," said Renee. Mom smiled, she was excited to see Renee so happy again.

Renee usually plays with her dolls until her mom walks in the room, which probably means it's time for bed. Finally, Mom opens the door and Renee shouts out, "Mom, this is how I want my hair tomorrow!". "Okay Babycakes, get ready for bed," said Mom.

As always, Renee said a prayer before bed. "Lord, thank you for showing me the beauty of my hair. Amen," prayed Renee.

Bright eyed and bushy tailed, Renee waltzed into Mom's bathroom for her morning routine. "Good morning Mom, I'm ready for my hairdo!" said Renee. Mom worked her magic and gave Renee the hairdo of her dreams! "Wow, my hair is AWESOME! My crown is polished and ready for school!" said Renee "Then let's get this Queen off to school!" smiled Mom.

Renee runs up the school steps
and sees her new friends.
"Your hair looks so cute Renee!" said Elaine.
"Yeah, I dig the fro!" said Robert.
"We all look good today,
we are FRO-TABULOUS!"

Guiding Questions and History

1. Can you relate to anyone in this book? If you can, how has that characters experience impacted you? If you can't, how will you push for change when you witness a situation like Renees?
2. How will you celebrate your differences?
3. How will you uplift and accept others' differences?
4. What does your hair mean to you?
5. I wrote this book because I felt that there was a problem that I wanted to solve. What problem do YOU see in the world that you want to change?

For many Black people, our hair holds our identity. It is how we feel in touch with those before us and express ourselves. After decades of being told we were less than, we decided to get back to our roots and indulge in our beauty. That is why I created this book for all of those kinked up, curly headed, melanated Kings and Queens.

9 780578 755762